This book belongs to:

Is That My Granny?

Written and Illustrated

by

Jennylynd James, Ph.D.

Copyright © 2018 Jennylynd James Enterprises
All rights reserved.

ISBN: 1727023927
ISBN-13: 978-1727023923

Published by Jennylynd James Enterprises
Toronto, Canada

JennylyndJames@gmail.com
http://jennylyndjames.com/books

DEDICATION

In loving memory of my mother, Gloria James who suffered from Alzheimer's disease. And also to my nephews who experienced their grandmother's transformation over the years as she succumbed to this disease.

My Granny lives alone in a house in Diamond Vale, Diego Martin.

She is big and tall, and very strong. My Granny grows fruits in the backyard and she loves to take care of her plants.

Granny hugs me when we go to visit her. She gives me sponge cake to eat and orange juice to drink.

Granny always gives me a big hug and a kiss on my cheeks.

One day, Granny pinched me and showed me an ugly face.

The next time I went to visit, she screamed at me and told me to stop talking.

Granny's mean. What has happened to my Granny?

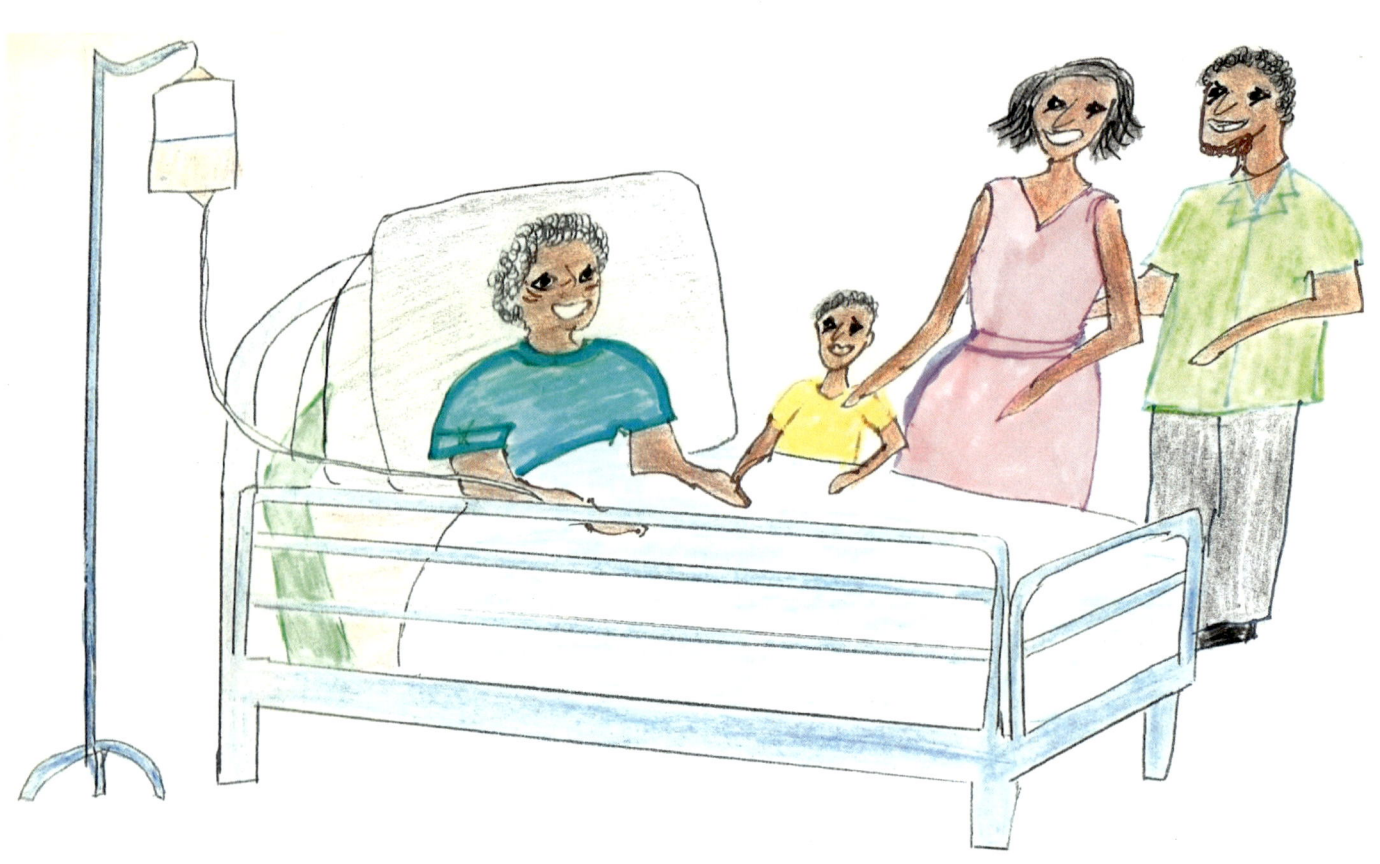

After that, Granny got sick and we went to see her in the hospital.

My mother said Granny would have to stay in another home.

Granny needed people to help her all the time.

We helped Granny pack her clothes. She went to live in a home with many other Grannies and Grandpas.

Soon after that, we went to visit her in the big new home.

Nurses walked around the big home feeding and helping all the Grannies and Grandpas.

Granny smiled when she saw us, but she forgot my name.

'Is that my Granny?' I asked my mother.

'She has Alzheimer's disease'.

'Alz... hei ... what? That's a really big word. I don't know how to spell that', I said.

'When people have Alzheimer's disease, they sometimes forget your name,' my mother said.

A long time after, we brought Granny home to our house to eat Christmas dinner with us.

Granny cannot walk. Now she has to sit in a wheel chair and we push her around.

Granny says the same thing over and over.

She called me Wallace and smiled.

'That's not my name, Granny. That's your brother's name.

Is that my Granny?' I asked.

'She has Alzheimer's disease and it will get worse,' said Mommy.

'It can get worse? That sounds scary,' I said.

After some months we visited Granny again, but she could not get out of bed.

She lay on the bed looking at us with sad eyes.

The nurse had to feed her.

She can't even go to the toilet. Granny wears big diapers like a baby.

The nurse has to change her diapers.

'Is that my Granny?' I asked.

'She is in the last stage of Alzheimer's Disease,' my mother said.

'Granny is just like a baby. She needs a lot of help.'

I felt very sad for my Granny and gave her a big hug.

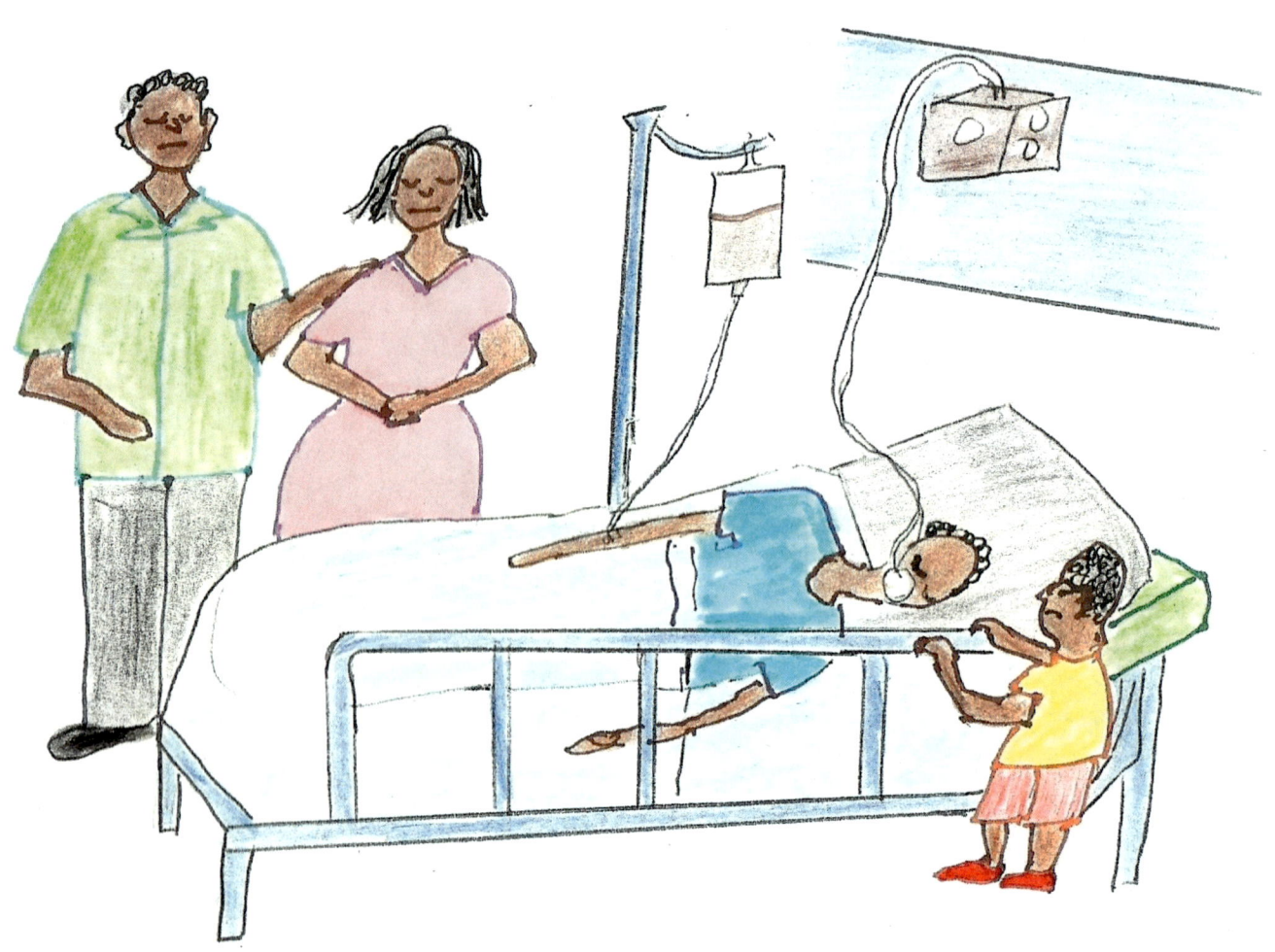

Not long after, my parents took me to the hospital.

Granny was lying on the bed with her eyes closed.

She could not speak, could not move and she had many tubes attached to her.

'Granny is really sick and won't be with us much longer,' said Daddy. 'Do you want to tell her goodbye?'

'But she can't hear me', I said.

'That's OK', said daddy. 'She will know you are here'.

I said goodbye to Granny and kissed her on her cheek.

I hope she heard me…

I saw Granny after that, at the big church. She was dressed up and looked like she was asleep, lying in a box.

'What box is this?' I asked Mommy.

'It's called a coffin,' she said. 'Granny is asleep forever.'

We all sang for Granny. Aunties, uncles, cousins and friends came to say goodbye.

Everyone cried.

But I didn't cry, because mommy said Granny is in a better place.

Bye Bye Granny.

We love you.

ABOUT THE BOOK

Alzheimer's disease is described as the progressive deterioration of the mind, personality and body, caused by the degeneration of the brain. The disease can begin in late middle age and continue into old age, but what starts the brain's deterioration is yet unknown. Learning about another family's journey can sometimes help in understanding and preparing, if your loved one is diagnosed with Alzheimer's disease. Every patient is affected by Alzheimer's disease differently, but the emotional rollercoaster is universal for caregivers and family members. This book, 'Is that My Granny?' is meant to address the emotions that small children experience in dealing with a grandparent who is afflicted with Alzheimer's disease. The child may find it confusing when a perfectly loving grandparent changes into an angry or quarrelsome individual. A child would also have difficulty understanding why his grandparent is in the hospital and unable to speak or unable to walk. Although Alzheimer's disease is a widespread affliction, parents may have challenges explaining the signs and symptoms of the disease to young children.

'Is that My Granny?' explores the phases in a grandmother's journey with Alzheimer's disease as observed through the eyes of a young boy. He must come to terms with the changes in his grandmother's body and character, and accept her eventual death. The book is loosely based on the experiences of my nephews with their grandmother who suffered with Alzheimer's for many years.

Photo: Jennylynd James with her mother, Gloria James

ABOUT THE AUTHOR

Jennylynd James is a 'Renaissance' woman: an artist, writer, and musician, with a long work history as a food scientist. Jennylynd earned a Ph.D. in food science at McGill University, Canada and worked in this field for over 20 years for large multinational companies in the United States, Ireland, and Canada. While living in Ireland she ran her own food processing business. When the Irish economy crashed on the heels of a worldwide recession, Jennylynd decided to fold up the business and move to Canada. Jennylynd lives in Toronto, Canada where she has embraced self expression in art, music, and writing as a new lifestyle. She has written a series of travel memoirs to chronicle her many adventures in relocation. Jennylynd experienced her mother's slow demise with Alzheimer's disease from 2006 to 2018. Other members in the family, like her nephews and daughter were puzzled by the changes in their grandmother's physical and mental state over the years. She wants her stories of resilience and thriving to empower and motivate readers.

http://jennylyndjames.com/books/

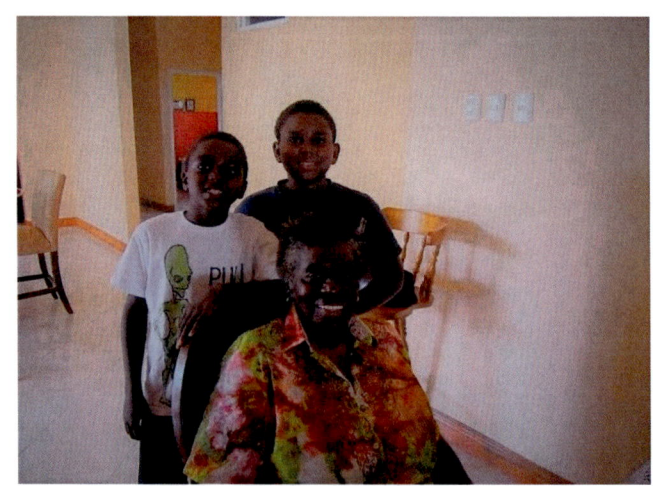

Photo: Nephews, Marcus and Nicholas with their Granny, Gloria James

Made in the USA
Columbia, SC
17 October 2018